THE SHERLOCK HOLMES

CHILDREN'S COLLECTION

MYSTERY, MISCHIEF AND MAYHEM

Published by Sweet Cherry Publishing Limited
Unit 36, Vulcan House,
Vulcan Road,
Leicester, LE5 3EF
United Kingdom

First published in the UK in 2020
2021 edition

2 4 6 8 10 9 7 5 3

ISBN: 978-1-78226-426-2

© Sweet Cherry Publishing

Sherlock Holmes: The Bruce-Partington Plans

Based on the original story from Sir Arthur Conan Doyle,
adapted by Stephanie Baudet.
Cover design by Arianna Bellucci and Rhiannon Izard
Illustrations by Arianna Bellucci

Lexile® code numerical measure L = Lexile® 600L

Guided Reading Level = W

www.sweetcherrypublishing.com

Printed and bound in India
I.TP002

SHERLOCK HOLMES
THE
BRUCE-PARTINGTON
PLANS

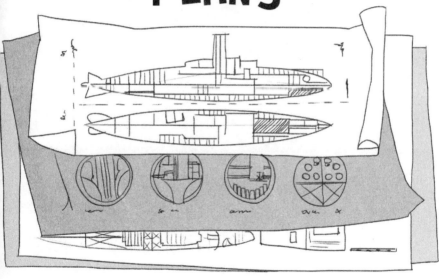

SIR ARTHUR CONAN DOYLE

Chapter One

This story begins in the third week of a cold November. A heavy fog had settled over London. From Monday to Thursday we could not see the houses across the road from our rooms in Baker Street.

On Monday, Holmes spent all day sorting out his papers. On Tuesday and Wednesday, he was busy with his latest hobby – studying the music of the Middle Ages. On Thursday, however, he had had enough.

We finished breakfast and peered miserably out of the windows. The heavy swirling fog was still drifting past. It left thick, oily drops on the windows.

I sat by the fire to read the newspaper, but Holmes would not join me. He hated doing nothing. He walked up and down our sitting room, biting his nails and tapping on the furniture.

'Is there anything interesting in the newspaper, Watson?' he said.

'There's news of a possible war and perhaps a change of government,' I replied, although I knew that he meant any interesting crimes.

He groaned in disgust and continued pacing.

'Criminals in London are dull people,' Holmes said in a whining voice.

'Look out of this window, Watson. You can only see a person for a second before they disappear into the fog again. A thief or a murderer could roam London today like a tiger in the jungle – silent and invisible.'

'There have been many small thefts, actually,' I said, still reading the newspaper.

Holmes snorted.

'It is lucky for London that I am not a criminal,' he said.

'It is, indeed,' I said.

'Imagine if I were a murderer.

I wonder how long I would survive if I were trying to track myself down. Hmm … Holmes the criminal against Holmes the detective … Oh, by Jove! Here comes something to break our boredom at last.'

It was Mrs Hudson with a telegram. Holmes tore it open and burst out laughing.

'Well, well, what next?' he said. 'My brother Mycroft is coming over.'

'Why is that surprising?' I asked.

'Why? Mycroft is like a tram, Watson. He runs around the same track and never goes anywhere else. Once, and only once, has he been here. What can possibly have derailed him?'

I had met Holmes' brother once. He was seven years older than Sherlock and nothing like him.

'Doesn't he say in his note?' I asked.

Holmes handed me the telegram.

Must see you about Cadogan West.
Coming at once.
Mycroft.

I looked up. 'Cadogan West. I have heard the name.'

'Well, it must be important,' said Holmes. 'For Mycroft to break his usual routine like this! It is like a dog deciding to walk on its hind legs. Did I ever tell you what Mycroft does?'

'You told me that he has a small job in the government,' I replied.

Holmes chuckled.

'Ah, well, yes. You are almost right. He does work for the British government. You would also be right if you said that he *is* the British government.'

'My dear Holmes!'

'I thought it might surprise you. Mycroft's job is very simple, yet the country could not do without him.'

'What is this mysterious job?' I asked Holmes. I put down my newspaper and leaned forwards, keen to hear the answer.

'Well, it's rather unique. You see, Mycroft has a great skill for storing facts. His brain is a little like my own. His job is to know everything about the government. The decisions made by each part of the government all go to him. So if a minister needs information about several subjects, Mycroft can focus on them all. He can say how each decision would affect the others. He has helped to make many important government decisions.

'He doesn't think of anything else but his job. Yet today he is coming here! What on earth can it mean? Who is Cadogan West, and what is he to Mycroft?'

I did not speak for a moment. I could not recall where I had heard this man's name. Then it struck me.

'I have it!' I cried, shuffling through a pile of newspapers. 'Yes, yes, here it is! Cadogan West was the young man who was found dead on the Underground on Tuesday morning.'

Holmes sat up and leaned forwards.

'This must be serious, Watson. Very serious indeed, if it has made Mycroft change his habits.'

'Well, at first, the papers said the young man simply fell out of a train and was killed,' I said. 'But now there has been an inquest, and many new facts have come out. I would say that it has become a very curious case, indeed.'

Holmes settled down in his armchair. 'All right, Watson, let us have the facts.'

Inquest

An inquest is made after someone has died or been murdered, to discover exactly what killed them. A coroner will look at the body and decide how the person died, then discuss it with other doctors and the police. I find these are often not needed – certainly not if I am on the case. I will have likely found the cause of death before the inquest is even held.

Chapter Two

I folded up my newspaper and put it on the table beside me.

'The man's name was Arthur Cadogan West,' I began. 'He was twenty-seven years old. He was a clerk at Woolwich Arsenal.'

'He worked for the government!' exclaimed Holmes. 'There is the link with my brother!'

'Cadogan West left Woolwich

suddenly on Monday night. The last person to see him was his fiancée, Miss Violet Westbury. He left her standing in the fog, at about seven-thirty that evening. She had no idea why. No one heard anything of him until his body was found. A railway worker called Mason discovered him,

Woolwich Arsenal

Also known as Royal Arsenal, this sector of the government works on top secret weaponry projects. They find, make and test the latest and most dangerous weapons in existence. Every person who works at Woolwich Arsenal knows that they must keep their work a secret – if information about the weapons got into the wrong hands, it could be extremely dangerous.

just outside Aldgate Station on the Underground system.'

'When?' asked Holmes.

'Six o'clock on the Tuesday morning. The body was lying away from the rails, on the left-hand side of the tracks. It was close to the station, right where the train line comes out of the tunnel. He had a bad head injury that must have been caused by the fall from the train. The body cannot have been carried down

from any nearby street. A ticket collector always stands at the station barriers, so he would have seen the murderer.'

Holmes looked at me, surprised. 'Very good, Watson! The case is plain enough. The man, dead or alive, either fell or was thrown from a train. That much is clear. Go on.'

'Well, the young man was definitely travelling late at night,' I added.

'But it is impossible to say where he got on the train.'

'His ticket would show that,' Holmes said.

'There was no ticket on him,' I replied.

'No ticket! Dear me, Watson, this is very strange. He would not have been able to reach the platform without showing a ticket. Cadogan West must have had one. Was it taken from him? Possibly. Or did he drop it in the carriage? That is also possible. But it is still strange. And there was no sign of robbery?'

'No. There is a list here of what he had on him.' I picked up the paper again and pointed.

His wallet contained two pounds fifteen shillings. He also had a cheque book for a bank in Woolwich, two tickets for a Monday evening show at Woolwich Theatre, and a small packet of important work documents.

Holmes seemed pleased.

'There we have it at last, Watson! British government – Woolwich Arsenal – important documents – my brother, Mycroft. It's all quite clear. Don't you think, Watson?'

'Um, well–' I stammered.

'Ah, and here comes Mycroft himself,' Holmes said, interrupting me.

A moment later Mycroft Holmes was shown into our room. He was a very big man, with a strong face and alert, steel-grey eyes.

Behind him came our old friend, Inspector Lestrade, of Scotland Yard. He was the opposite to Mycroft – slim and stern. I could see by the expression on both their faces that this case was very serious. The detective shook our hands without a word. Mycroft Holmes took off his overcoat and sank into an armchair.

'This is a most annoying business, Sherlock,' he said. 'I really hate changing my habits, but it couldn't be helped. I have never seen the Prime Minister so upset. The Admiralty is buzzing like an overturned beehive! Have you read about the case?'

'We have just done so. What were the important documents?'

'Luckily the answer to that has not come out in the newspapers'

Admiralty

This part of the government is in command of the Royal Navy. The Admiralty is made up of a group of very powerful and important people – they have control over all affairs at sea and help plan the Royal Navy's war tactics.

Mycroft said, shaking his head. 'They are top secret. The papers were the plans of the Bruce-Partington submarine.'

Mycroft looked at Sherlock and I. 'Surely you have heard of it?' he asked. 'I thought everyone had.'

'Only as a name,' said Sherlock.

'It is a carefully guarded government secret. The Bruce-Partington submarine is an extremely powerful weapon. The plans are very complicated. There are more than thirty separate sections. These plans were kept in a safe, in a private office at Woolwich Arsenal. The office had burglar-proof doors and windows.

'The plans were never meant to be taken outside the office. And yet, here we find them – in the pocket of a dead junior clerk, in the middle of London.'

'But you got them back?'

'No, Sherlock, no! That's the point. We have not. Ten papers were taken from Woolwich but there were only seven in Cadogan West's pocket. The three most important papers are gone! You must drop everything, Sherlock. Never mind your little police puzzles.'

I caught the sorry look that Sherlock gave Lestrade.

'Why don't you solve it yourself, Mycroft?' Sherlock asked.

'I could, Sherlock. But it is a question of getting details. Find me the details, and from an armchair I will put them together and give you the answer. But to run here and there, question people, and lie on the floor with a magnifying glass to my eye – it is not my thing. No, you are the man to clear the matter up. If you fancy seeing your name on the next honours list that is ...'

My friend smiled and shook his head.

'I play the game for the game's own sake,' Holmes said. 'But this case has some interesting points.

I will be very pleased to look into it. Some more facts, please.'

'I have written down the important ones on this paper. There are a few addresses, too, that you will find helpful. The real guardian of the papers is Sir James Walter. He is an honest man, who has been in the service for many years. He is one of two people who have a key to the safe.'

'Who was the other man with a key?' Holmes asked.

'The senior clerk, Mr Sidney Johnson. He is a man of forty,

married, with five children. He says that he was at home the whole of Monday evening. His wife agrees. His key has never left his watch chain.'

Sherlock paused. 'Tell us about Cadogan West,' he said.

'He has been in the service for ten years and has done good work. His work meant that he used the Bruce-Partington plans every day. No one else handled them.'

'Well, surely it is clear who took them, then? It was the junior clerk, Cadogan West – they were found on his body. That seems final, doesn't it?'

Mycroft nodded. 'It does, Sherlock. But, why did he take them?'

'Were they valuable?' asked Holmes.

'He could have sold them for several thousand pounds,' Mycroft replied.

'Well then, surely Cadogan West took the papers to sell them. He must have had a copy of the key …'

'Of several keys, actually,' said Mycroft. 'He had to open the building and then the room and then the safe.'

'So, he had several keys copied. Then he took the papers to London to sell the secret. He was going to put them back in the safe before anyone noticed. But in the middle of his journey back, someone killed him.'

'It's possible,' said Mycroft. 'Yet you miss out a lot, Sherlock. If Cadogan West *had* meant to take the papers to London, then he would have made an appointment with the foreign agent he was selling them to. He would not have bought two tickets for the theatre, taken his fiancée halfway there, and then suddenly disappeared.'

'A trick,' said Lestrade, who had been listening impatiently to the conversation.

Sherlock raised his eyebrows. 'A very strange one. That is point number one. Point number two: what happened to the other three papers? And where is the money the foreign agent would have paid him for the secrets? We should have found a large sum of money in his pocket.'

'It seems perfectly clear to me,' said Lestrade. 'Cadogan West took the papers to sell them. He saw the agent. They could not agree on a price. He set off home again, but the agent followed him. In the train, the agent murdered West. He took the more important papers off him, and left the other seven. Then he threw West's body off the train. That would explain everything, wouldn't it?'

'Why didn't he have a ticket?' asked Holmes.

'The agent would have taken it, so no one could find out where they met.'

'Good, Lestrade, very good,' said Sherlock. 'But if this is true, then the case is solved. The traitor is dead and the plans for the Bruce-Partington submarine have already been smuggled away. What is there for us to do?'

'To act, Sherlock – to act!' cried Mycroft, springing to his feet. 'I don't agree with this explanation.

Use your powers! Go to the scene of the crime! See the people involved! Leave no stone unturned! In all your career you have never had such a great chance of serving your country.'

'Well, well,' said Holmes, shrugging. 'Come then, Watson. And you, Lestrade. Could you come with us? We will go to Aldgate Station, where the body was found. Goodbye, Mycroft. I shall give you a report tonight.'

Chapter Three

An hour later, Holmes, Lestrade and
I were standing on the Underground
railway track, just before Aldgate
Station. A polite, red-faced railway
worker was helping us.

'This is where the young man's
body was found,' he said,
pointing to a
spot beside
the tracks.

'It could only have fallen from a train. There was one that passed just before midnight on Monday.'

'Have the carriages been examined for any signs of a fight?' asked Holmes.

'Yes. There are no clues that there was a fight on board. No ticket has been found, either.'

'Were any doors left open?'

'No,' replied the railway worker. 'Whatever is the matter with Mr Holmes?'

Holmes was standing, staring at the railway tracks.

'Points,' he muttered. 'The points.'

'What do you mean?' I asked.

He turned to the railwayman. 'I suppose there aren't many stations with this many points?'

The man shook his head. 'No, not many.'

'And a curve too. Points, and a curve. By Jove!'

'What is it, Mr Holmes? Have you found a clue?' asked Lestrade.

Points

The points on a railway track allow the train to move from one track to another. Usually, one larger railway track will come up to a point and then split into two smaller tracks. This will commonly create a Y shape. Points and curves in a track can make the train judder and sway as it moves past them.

'Not really a clue, more an idea. But the case has certainly become more interesting. Unique even. Perfectly unique, and yet why not? I do not see any sign of blood on the line.'

'There was hardly any,' said Lestrade.

'But I thought there were serious injuries,' I interrupted.

'Yes, but no visible wounds,' said the inspector.

'I would have expected some bleeding. Would it be possible for me to have a look at the train that you said passed just before midnight?' asked Holmes.

The railwayman shook his head. 'I'm afraid not, Mr Holmes. The train has been broken up and the carriages were put on other trains.'

'I promise you, Mr Holmes, that every carriage has been carefully examined. I saw to it myself,' said Lestrade.

Holmes turned away. 'As it happens, it was not the carriages that I wanted to examine,' he snapped. 'Watson, we have done all we can here. We will not trouble you any further, Mr Lestrade. I think our investigation must now take us to Woolwich.'

Chapter Four

Holmes wrote a telegram to his brother, and he handed it to me before sending it.

I think I know where to go next, but I could be going in the wrong direction. Please send me a list of the addresses of all foreign spies known to be in England.
Sherlock.

'That should be helpful, Watson,' he said as we took our seats on the Woolwich train. 'We must thank Mycroft for introducing us to this remarkable case.'

Holmes was certainly very different from this morning. Gone was the bored and miserable man, who paced about our sitting room in his dressing gown. Here

was the Holmes I knew. The detective; the adventurer!

'There are clues here,' he said. 'I should have seen them earlier. I think, Watson, that Cadogan West met his death elsewhere. I believe his body was placed on the *roof* of a carriage.'

'On the roof!' I cried.

'Strange, isn't it? But think about the facts. The body was found at the very place where the train sways and wobbles as it comes around the bend. Surely that is exactly where something that was put on the roof would fall off?

'Just think about it,' he continued. 'It makes sense that there is no blood on the line if the body bled elsewhere.'

'And the ticket!'

'Exactly, Watson. We could not explain why there was no ticket. Perhaps it's because he was already dead – a dead man does not buy a ticket. Everything fits together.'

'But even if that is all true, we still do not know how or why he was killed,' I said.

'That is true,' said Holmes, thoughtfully. He fell into a daydream that lasted until the train drew up in Woolwich Station. There he called a cab and took Mycroft's notes from his pocket. 'We have quite a few calls to make this afternoon,' Holmes said, gazing down at the notepaper. 'I think that Sir James Walter should be the first.'

The famous official's house was a fine villa, with green lawns that stretched down to the River Thames. As we reached it, the fog was lifting and a thin, watery sunshine was breaking through.

Holmes asked the cab to wait. We walked up to the front door and rang the bell.

A butler answered.

'Sir James, sir!' he said, with a sad, serious face. 'Sir James died this morning.'

'Good heavens!' cried Holmes. 'How did he die?'

'Perhaps you would like to come in, sir? You can speak to his brother, Colonel Valentine?'

'Yes, we had better do that,' replied Holmes.

We were shown into a dimly lit drawing room. A very tall, handsome, light-bearded man of fifty walked in after us. He was the younger brother of Sir James.

Colonel Valentine's wild eyes, tear-stained cheeks and messy hair showed his sadness at his brother's death. He even had difficulty speaking.

'It was this horrible scandal,' he said. 'My brother, Sir James, was always so proud of how well his department was run. The shame of the scandal broke his heart.'

'We had hoped that he might give us some information to help solve the mystery,' said Holmes. 'Do you happen to know anything else about the affair?'

Colonel Valentine shook his head. 'I don't know anything except what I have read or heard. I don't want to be rude, Mr Holmes, but I'm sure you can understand that we are very sad at the moment. I must ask you to leave us alone.'

We left at once and climbed back into the cab.

'I certainly did not expect that,' said my friend, settling into the seat. 'I wonder if the death was natural or whether there was something criminal about it.

Could Sir James have played a part in this mystery? We must leave that question for the future. Now we shall go to the Cadogan Wests.'

The mother of Arthur Cadogan West lived in a small but tidy house, just outside Woolwich. She was too sad and confused to help us, but sitting beside her was Miss Violet Westbury, the dead man's fiancée. She was the last person to see him on that fatal night.

'I can't explain it, Mr Holmes,' Miss Violet said. 'I have not slept at all since the night Arthur died.

I have been thinking and thinking, night and day, what the truth could be. Arthur was the most determined, loyal, honest man on earth. He would have cut off his right hand before he would sell a state secret. Anyone who knew him would tell you that.'

'But the facts, Miss Westbury?' said Holmes.

'Yes, yes, I admit that I cannot explain them.'

'Did he need money?'

'No. He never needed much. His pay was enough to cover the bills. He had even saved a few hundred pounds. We were to going to get married next year.'

'Did he seem like his usual self?' Holmes asked. 'Please, tell us the truth.'

Her face flushed red and she paused for a moment.

'Well,' she said at last. 'I had a feeling that there was something on his mind.'

'For how long?'

'Only for the last week or so. I asked him about it. He said that there was something, and that it was about his work. But he never said anything more.'

Holmes looked serious.

'Come on, Miss Westbury. We need all the details, even if they seem to blame him. It may lead us to the truth.'

'I have nothing more to tell.

Once or twice I thought he was about to tell me the secret. But he never did. He only said that foreign spies would pay a lot to have it.'

My friend looked even more serious.

'Anything else?'

'He said that the government was careless about such matters,' Miss Westbury said. 'He thought that it would be easy for a traitor to get the plans.'

'When did he say this?' Holmes asked.

'Not long ago.'

'Now tell us about that last evening,' said Holmes.

I saw sadness swim into her eyes. I felt sorry for her.

'We were going to the theatre. The fog was so thick that we had to walk instead of getting a cab. Our walk took us close to the Woolwich office. Suddenly Arthur dashed away.'

'Without a word?'

'He just shouted "Good heavens!", and then ran away. I waited for him, but he never came back. Then I walked home. The next morning, after the office opened, the government workers came to ask where he was. At about twelve o'clock, we heard the terrible news. Oh, Mr Holmes, surely he is not guilty?'

Homes simply shrugged and shook his head sadly.

'Come, Watson,' he said. 'Our next stop must be the office.'

Chapter Five

When we were back in the carriage, Holmes turned to me. 'Things looked bad for Cadogan West before,' he said. 'But this new information makes it even worse. He has motive. If he was getting married soon, then he would want a little extra money. He was even talking about stealing the plans, right before they were stolen! It is all very bad.'

'But surely, Holmes, character goes for something? He was a good man, it seems. Also, why should he leave the girl in the street while he went to commit the crime?'

'Exactly! There are still many things to explain,' replied Holmes.

Mr Sidney Johnson, the senior clerk, met us at the office. He was a thin, gruff, middle-aged man with glasses. His cheeks were haggard, and his hands twitched nervously.

'It is bad, Mr Holmes, very bad! Have you heard that Sir Walter is dead?'

'We have just come from his house,' said Holmes.

'The place is in chaos!' cried Mr Johnson. 'The boss is dead, Cadogan West is dead, and our papers are stolen. And yet, when we closed our door on Monday evening, everything was in order.

Good gracious! I'm shocked that West, of all men, should have done such a thing!'

'You are sure he is guilty, then?' asked Holmes.

'I can see no other explanation,' said Mr Johnson.

'What time did the office close on Monday?' asked Holmes.

'At five,' replied Johnson.

'Did you close it?'

The clerk nodded. 'I am always the last man out.'

'Where were the Bruce-Partington plans?'

'In the safe. I put them there myself.'

'Is there a watchman in the building?'

'There is, but he has lots of rooms to guard. He is an old soldier and a very trustworthy man,' said Johnson. 'He saw nothing that evening. I am not surprised – the fog was very thick.'

'If Cadogan West wanted to steal the papers, he would need three keys, wouldn't he?' asked Holmes.

'Yes, he would. The key for the outer door, the key for the office, and the key to open the safe.'

'Only Sir James Walter and you had those keys?'

'I did not have keys to the doors, only the key for the safe.'

Holmes thought for a moment. 'Was Sir James a tidy man?'

'Yes, I think he was. I know that he kept those three keys on the same key ring.'

'And he took that key ring to London?'

'He said so,' replied Johnson.

'And your key never left your possession?'

'Never.'

'Then Cadogan West must have had copies made,' said Holmes. 'And yet none were found on his body. It seems that every enquiry in this case brings me a new mystery. Now there are three papers still missing. I understand that they are the important ones.'

'Yes, that's right,' said Johnson.

'Do you mean to say that anyone holding these three papers could construct a Bruce-Partington submarine? Even without the other seven papers?'

'That is what I told the Admiralty. But today I have been over the drawings again, and I am not so sure of it. A key part of the submarine is drawn on one of the seven papers that have been returned. Without that part, the thieves cannot make the submarine.'

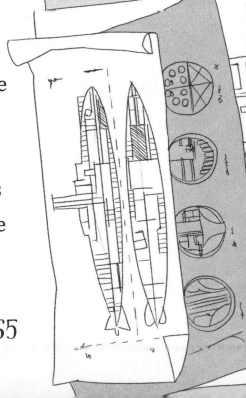

'But the three missing drawings are the most important?' asked Holmes.

'Certainly,' said Johnson.

'May we take a walk around the rooms?'

Holmes examined the lock of the safe, the door of the room, and the iron shutters of the window. When we walked outside onto the lawn, Holmes suddenly became very excited.

There was a laurel bush outside the office's window. Several of the bush's branches were twisted or snapped. Holmes inspected them with his magnifying glass. Then he peered down at some faint marks on the soil, beneath. Finally, he asked the chief clerk to close the shutters. They hardly met in the centre. It seemed anyone standing outside the office would have clearly seen what was going on inside the room.

'It may mean something or it may not,' Holmes muttered to himself. 'But I do not think we will find anything more in Woolwich. Let's see if we can do better in London.'

But Woolwich did have a little more to offer. The clerk in the train station's ticket office told us that he was sure he saw Cadogan West on the Monday night. He got on the eight-fifteen train. He was alone and bought a single third-class ticket. The clerk knew him well and noticed that he was excited and nervous. He was so shaky that he could hardly pick up his change.

We looked at the timetable. The eight-fifteen was the first train that Cadogan West could have taken after he left his fiancée at about seven-thirty.

'Let us put this all together, Watson,' said Holmes, after half an hour of sitting on the train in silence. 'Surely, we have made *some* progress.

'Our enquiries in Woolwich have mainly made Cadogan West look guilty. But it still does not quite add up. Say a foreign agent did offer him a secret deal.

Now imagine that Cadogan West was on his way to the theatre with Miss Westbury. He's walking past the office when he sees this same agent walking towards the building. Curious, West followed the man. Through the gap in the window shutters, he saw the agent take the documents. Then he followed the thief. That's why Cadogan West did not make copies of the plans – because he was not the one who stole them.'

Chapter Six

'What is the next step?' I asked as we reached Baker Street Station.

'Well, here we come into difficulties,' replied Holmes. 'You would think that Cadogan West would seize the villain and call the police. Why didn't he do that? Could the thief have been his boss? That would explain why he would not have called the police on him.

Or could the thief have disappeared in the fog? Perhaps Cadogan West ran through London to catch the agent at his home; if he knew where the home was, that is. He must have thought it was a very urgent and serious situation. He would not have left Miss Westbury standing in the fog if it were not. He did not even take a second to tell her where he was going.

'Our trail runs cold here,' went on Holmes as we walked towards our flat. 'And there is a big gap. Even if our theory is correct, we still do not know how West's body ended up on the roof of a train, with seven papers in his pocket. My plan now is to work from the other end. If Mycroft has given us the foreign agents' addresses, then we may be able to find our man.'

Sure enough, a note was waiting for us at Baker Street. Holmes looked at it quickly and threw it over to me.

There are many foreign agents in London, but few who would handle such a big job. The only men worth investigating are:

- Adolph Meyer,
  13 Great George Street, Westminster
- Louis la Rothiere,
  Camden Mansions, Notting Hill
- Hugo Oberstein,
  13 Caulfield Gardens, Kensington

The last one was known to be in London on Monday. It seems he has now left. Glad you are making progress. The Cabinet is keen to hear your report. Some very important people have arrived from the highest part of the government. The whole force of the country is behind you if you should need it.

Mycroft

Holmes smiled. 'I'm afraid that all the queen's horses and all the queen's men cannot help in this matter.'

I smiled too. Although, the pressure on Holmes to solve the problem seemed impossible.

He spread out his big map of London and leaned over it.

'Well, well,' he said after a while. 'Things are looking better. Why, Watson, I do believe that we are going to pull it off after all.'

He slapped me on the

shoulder. 'I am going out now. Only for a quick inspection. I will do nothing serious without you, my trusted comrade. You stay here and I will be back again in an hour or two. If you get bored, get a paper and pen and begin your story of how we saved the country.'

For Holmes to be the opposite of his usual serious manner meant that he must be onto something. All that long November evening I waited impatiently for him to come back.

At last, just after nine o'clock, a messenger arrived with a note.

Am at Goldini's Restaurant, Gloucester Road, Kensington. Please come at once. Bring a jemmy, a lantern, a chisel and a gun. S.H.

'Wonderful,' I muttered to myself sarcastically. 'These are just the type of tools a respectable doctor should be carrying through the dim, foggy streets of London!'

I tutted and sighed, but, eventually, did exactly as Holmes

Jemmy

A short, heavy metal bar that is used to break open locked windows or doors. Most burglars will carry a jemmy and use it to break into the homes of rich people, and steal whatever treasures they find there.

asked. I carefully hid each item in the pockets of my overcoat, then got a cab straight to the address. There was my friend, sitting at a little round table near the door of the Italian restaurant.

'Have you had something to eat?' he asked.

When I nodded he said, 'Then join me for a coffee. Have you got the tools?'

'They are here, in my overcoat.'

'Excellent. Let me catch you up. Now, be clear, Watson, that this young man's body was *placed* on the roof of the train. That is obvious.'

'Couldn't he have been dropped from a bridge?' I asked.

'That would be impossible. If you look at the roofs you will see that they are slightly rounded, and there is no railing around them. So Cadogan West's body would have instantly fallen or bounced off. Therefore, we can say for certain he was placed on it.'

'How could he have been put there?'

'That was the question we had to answer. There is only one possible way. You know that the Underground tracks run outside the tunnels in some places in the West End? Well, when I last travelled that way, I remember seeing windows just above my head. They were the windows of houses, that lined the side of the train track. Now, suppose that a train stopped under such a window, would it be difficult to lay a body on the roof?'

'It seems unlikely.'

'Yes, that may be so. But there is an old saying, Watson: when every other theory fails, whatever remains, however unlikely, must be the truth. Here, all other possibilities *have* failed. I think you were a little surprised at my excitement when I saw Mycroft's list of addresses. It was because of the spy – the big international spy who had just left London. He lived in the row of houses next to the Underground.'

'Oh, that was it, was it?'

'Yes, that was it. Mr Hugo Oberstein, of 13, Caulfield Gardens. He has become the key person in my investigation. I began at Gloucester Road Station. A very helpful railway man walked with me along the track. I had to be sure that the rear windows of Caulfield Gardens back onto the line. They do. Even more important is the fact that the trains stop. Because there are so many trains crossing paths, some Underground trains have to stop for several minutes at that very spot.'

'Wonderful, Holmes! You have
got it!' I cried.

'So far, Watson, we are making progress, but the goal is still far off.

'Well, after I had seen the back of Caulfield Gardens, I walked round to the front. I was sure that the man had definitely left. It is a large house, and Oberstein lived there with just one personal servant and a few maids. The personal servant was probably in on the whole thing. We must remember that Hugo Oberstein has gone to the Continent to sell stolen goods. It was not to escape the police. He had no reason to fear a police search on his house and an amateur search would never occur to him. Yet, that is exactly what we are going to do.'

'Could we not get a search warrant and make it legal?' I begged.

'Not with the little evidence we have,' replied Holmes.

'What could we possibly find there?'

'There may be some letters.'

'I don't like it, Holmes.'

'My dear fellow, you shall keep watch in the street. I'll do the criminal part. It's not a time to overthink things. Remember Mycroft's note, and the Admiralty, and the Cabinet, and the Prime Minister who waits for news. We must go.'

I got up from the table.

'You are right, Holmes. We must go.'

He sprang up and shook me by the hand.

'I knew you would not refuse,' he said. For a moment I saw a fond, caring expression in his eyes. The next instant he was back to busily making plans.

'It is nearly half a mile, but there is no hurry. We can walk,' he said. 'Please do not drop the tools. It would be very unlucky if you were arrested *before* we break into the house.'

Chapter Seven

Caulfield Gardens was a row of flat-fronted Victorian houses. Next door, there seemed to be a children's party going on. The merry buzz of young voices and the clatter of a piano echoed through the night.

The fog still hung about and hid us with its friendly shade. Holmes had lit his lantern and held it in front of the massive door.

'This is a problem,' he said. 'It
is bolted as well as locked. The
basement door might be easier. Plus,
there is an archway down there where
we can hide, in case anyone should
walk by. Give me a hand, Watson.'

A minute later we were over
the railings and standing by the
basement. We slid into the shadow
of the archway just in time to avoid
being seen by a policeman. His heavy

footsteps crossed the front of the house and then slowly died away. Holmes set to work on the door. I watched him stoop and strain until, with a sharp crash, it flew open.

He hurried through and I followed, though my mind was telling me not to. We were in a dark passage. I closed the door behind us. Holmes led the way up the curving, uncarpeted stairs. We walked into a room and the light from Holmes' lantern reflected off a dirty window.

'Here we are, Watson – this must be the one.'

He threw the window open. As he did so, there was a low, harsh murmur. The sound grew into a loud roar as a train dashed past us in the darkness. It sent steam and smoke billowing into the room.

Holmes shone his light along the windowsill. It was thickly coated with soot from the passing engines. But the black surface was smudged in places.

'You can see where they rested the body. Now, Watson, what's this? It is definitely a blood mark.' He was pointing to a faint smudge of colour along the woodwork of the window. 'Let us stay here until a train stops.'

We did not have long to wait. The next train roared from the tunnel, but then slowed and

screeched to a stop right under us.
It was so close that we could almost
touch the roof of the carriage.

Holmes softly closed the window.

'So far we are correct. What do
you think, Watson?'

'A masterpiece. You have done
very well, Holmes.'

He gave a small smile and shook
his head. 'I cannot agree with you
there, my dear fellow. From the
moment that I had the idea of the

body being on the roof, all the rest
was clear. If this were a normal case,
our work would be over. But, as it is,
problems still lie ahead.'

He had climbed the kitchen stairs
and gone into some rooms on the
first floor. One was a dining room. It
was a little drab, cold and contained
nothing of interest. The second was
Hugo Oberstein's bedroom. That
did not hold any clues, either. The
third room seemed more promising.
Holmes began to examine it carefully.
It was littered with books and papers
and was obviously used as a study.

Holmes rifled through drawer after drawer and cupboard after cupboard. But there was no smile of success to brighten his serious face. After a full hour, we had no more clues than when we started.

'The cunning dog has covered his tracks,' Holmes said. 'This is our last chance.'

He pointed to a small tin cashbox on the writing desk. He picked it up and prised it open with his chisel. Inside were several rolls of paper covered with numbers and sums. But there was no note to explain what they meant. The words "water pressure" and "pressure to the square inch" sounded like something to do with submarines. But I couldn't be sure. Holmes tossed them aside impatiently. All that was left was an envelope with some small newspaper clippings inside it. He shook them out onto the table, and at once I saw his face brighten. This must be a clue.

'What's this, Watson? What's this?' he asked, merrily. 'A series of messages hidden in newspaper advertisements. Looks like the *Daily Telegraph*'s personal column by the print and type of paper. No dates, but this must be the first.

Hoped to hear sooner. Terms agreed to. Write fully to address given on card. Pierott.

'Next comes:

Too complex for description.
Must have full report.
Stuff awaits you when
goods delivered. Pierott.

'Finally:

Monday night after nine. Two
taps. Only ourselves. Do not be
so suspicious. Payment in cash
when goods delivered. Pierott.

'A complete record, Watson! If we
only knew who he wrote these to.'

He sat lost in thought, tapping
his fingers on the table. Finally, he
sprang to his feet.

'Perhaps it won't be so difficult, after all! Come, Watson, let us drive round to the offices of the *Daily Telegraph*. Let's bring a good day's work to an end.'

Chapter Eight

The next morning after breakfast, Mycroft and Lestrade came round. Holmes told them what wc had done the previous day. The inspector shook his head when we mentioned the burglary.

'We can't do these things in the police force, Mr Holmes,' he said. 'No wonder you get results that are beyond us. But one of these days you'll go too far, and you'll find yourself and your friend in trouble.'

Holmes tutted. 'Defenders of our country, eh, Watson? But what do you think of it, Mycroft?'

'Excellent, Sherlock! Admirable! But what will you do with the clues you have found?'

Holmes picked up the *Daily Telegraph* that lay on the table.

'Have you seen Pierrot's advertisement for today?'

'What? Another one?' asked Mycroft.

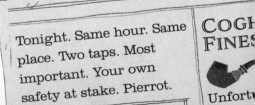

Tonight. Same hour. Same place. Two taps. Most important. Your own safety at stake. Pierrot.

COGH
FINES

Unfort

'Yes, here it is.'

'By George!' cried Lestrade. 'If he answers that we've got him!'

'That was my idea when I put it in. Can you both come with us to Caulfield Gardens tonight? At about eight o'clock? I think we might solve our mystery tonight.'

Lestrade and Mycroft had agreed to meet us outside Gloucester Road Station. The basement door of Hugo Oberstein's house had been left unlocked the night before. I had to go in and open the front door because Mycroft absolutely refused to climb the railings.

By nine o'clock we were all seated in the study, waiting patiently for our man.

An hour passed, and then another. When eleven o'clock struck, the chime of the great church clock seemed to mark the end of our hopes. Lestrade and Mycroft were fidgeting in their seats and looking at their watches every thirty seconds. Holmes was silent and calm. Suddenly, he raised his head with a jerk.

'He is coming,' he said.

We heard a quiet, creeping step, shuffling and then two sharp taps with the knocker.

Holmes stood up, signing to us to stay seated. He walked to the door, opened it and welcomed in the dark figure. The figure slipped past him, as silently as a shadow, and Holmes closed the door again.

'This way!' we heard Holmes say. A moment later our man stood before us.

The man turned with a cry of surprise when he saw us. He went to run, but Holmes caught him by the collar and threw him back into the room. Within seconds, the door was shut and Holmes was standing with his back against it.

The man glared around him, staggered, and then fell unconscious onto the floor. His broad-brimmed hat flew from his head and his scarf slipped from his neck. There, beneath the layers of material, was the long, light beard and the soft, handsome face of Colonel Valentine Walter.

Holmes gave a whistle of surprise.

'Well, Watson,' he said. 'This was not the man that I was expecting.'

Chapter Nine

'Who is he?' asked
Mycroft, eagerly.

'The younger brother
of the late Sir James
Walter,' Holmes replied.
'The same Sir James
who was the head of the
Submarine Department.

Now I understand. He is waking up. Please let me question him.'

We carried him to the sofa. Our prisoner sat up and looked around in horror. He put his hand to his forehead.

'What is this?' he asked. 'I came here to visit Mr Oberstein.'

'We know everything, Colonel Walter,' said Holmes. 'I cannot understand how an English gentleman could behave as you have done. We know about all your dealings with Oberstein. We also know how young

Cadogan West died. We would think a little better of you if you confessed and looked a bit sorry.'

The man groaned and sank his face into his hands. We waited, but he was silent.

'Do not deny it,' said Holmes. 'We know that you needed money, and that you made copies of your brother's keys. We know that you contacted Oberstein, the spy. He answered your letters through the personal columns of the *Daily Telegraph*. You went to the Arsenal office in the fog on Monday night. Cadogan West saw you and followed you. He saw your theft but could not call the police, because he thought you may have been taking the papers to your brother. Leaving his fiancée alone in the fog, he followed you, like the good citizen he was. He kept right behind you until you reached this very house. There he accused you, so you killed him. You killed an innocent man.'

'I did not! I did not! I swear that I did not!' cried the colonel.

'Tell us, then, how Cadogan West died before you laid him on the roof of a railway carriage.'

'I will. I swear to you that I will. I did the rest. I confess it. It was just as you say. I needed money, badly. Oberstein offered me five thousand pounds to steal the plans. But I did not murder Cadogan West.'

'What happened, then?' asked Holmes.

'Cadogan West was suspicious and he followed me back here. Because of the fog, though, I did not see him until I was at the door.

I knocked and Oberstein opened the door. West rushed up from behind me and demanded to know what we were doing with the papers. Oberstein had his walking stick. As Cadogan West forced his way into the house, Oberstein struck him on the head with it. He was dead within five minutes. His body was just lying there in the hall. We did not know what to do. Then Oberstein had this idea about the trains that stopped under his back window. But first he looked at the Bruce-

Partington papers. He said that he needed to keep three of them.

'"You cannot keep them," I said. "If we do not return them to Woolwich, the government will know they have been stolen. They will be on our heels quicker than flies to honey."

'"I must keep them," he said. "They are so complicated that it is impossible to make copies of them."

'"No, they must *all* go back tonight," I said.

'He thought for a while and then said, "I will keep three. We can stuff the others into this man's pockets. Then it will all be blamed on him."

'I could see no other way out of it, so I agreed. We waited half an hour at the window before a train stopped. The fog was so thick that no one could see what we were doing. We lowered West's body onto the train, and that was the end of the matter. Well, I thought it was.'

'And Sir James?' Holmes asked.

'My brother said nothing. But I think that he suspected me. He died from the shame – the shame I caused him.'

There was silence in the room. It was broken by Mycroft Holmes.

'Can you not make up for what you've done? It would ease your conscience and perhaps you would get a lighter sentence.'

'How can I do that?' asked Colonel Walter.

'Where is Oberstein with the papers?' Mycroft replied.

'I don't know.'

'Didn't he give you an address?'

'He told me to send letters to the Hotel de Louvre, Paris.'

'Then you can still put things right,' said Holmes.

'I will do anything I can. I owe Oberstein nothing. He has been my ruin and my downfall,' said the colonel.

'Here is some paper and a pen. Sit at this desk and write what I say,' said Holmes. 'Put the address you gave me on the envelope.'

Walter sat at the table and we all watched as he wrote.

Dear Sir,

You will have noticed by now that one important detail is missing from the plans. I have that detail. Getting this final piece of the puzzle has put me in great danger. I must ask you for another five hundred pounds. I will not trust it to the post, nor will I take anything but gold or notes in payment. I would come to you abroad, but it would look strange if I left the country now. Therefore, I shall meet you in the smoking room of the Charing Cross Hotel at noon on Saturday.

'That will do very well,' said Holmes. 'I would be very surprised if that does not fetch our man.'

And it did! Oberstein was fooled by the trick. He arrived at the hotel, was arrested, and got fifteen years in prison. In his luggage we found the Bruce-Partington plans. He had put them up for auction all over Europe.

Colonel Walter was also sent to prison. He died there, in the second year of his sentence.

Some weeks after the case was over, Holmes took a trip to

Windsor Castle. He returned with a very fine emerald tiepin. He said that it was a present from someone very special, to thank him for his work.

He said no more, but I think I can guess the great lady's name. After all, a tiepin like that is unlikely to come from anyone less than Her Majesty herself.

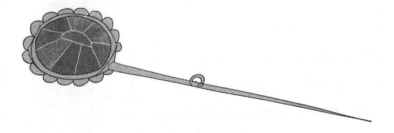

Sherlock Holmes

World-renowned private detective Sherlock Holmes has solved hundreds of mysteries, and is the author of such fascinating monographs as *Early English Charters* and *The Influence of a Trade Upon the Form of a Hand.* He keeps bees in his free time.

Dr John Watson

Wounded in action at Maiwand, Dr John Watson left the army and moved into 221B Baker Street. There he was surprised to learn that his new friend, Sherlock Holmes, faced daily peril solving crimes, and began documenting his investigations. Dr Watson also runs a doctor's practice.

To download Sherlock Holmes activities, please visit www.sweetcherrypublishing.com/resources